About the Author

Saja Ibrahim was born in the United States, lived and grew up in Saudi Arabia. Her ancestors are of different origins, which allowed for her exposure to various cultures and traditions. She completed her bachelor's in marketing, studies yoga, and philosophy. The first novel she read was found on her grandmother's bed stand when she was a teenager, and she has not stopped reading since. She writes today in hopes that somewhere in her stories we find a way to leave the world a better place than the one we received.

Look, It's a Monkey!

Saja Ibrahim

Look, It's a Monkey!

Olympia Publishers
London

www.olympiapublishers.com
OLYMPIA PAPERBACK EDITION

Copyright © Saja Ibrahim 2024

The right of Saja Ibrahim to be identified as author of
this work has been asserted in accordance with sections 77 and 78 of
the Copyright, Designs and Patents Act 1988.

All Rights Reserved

No reproduction, copy or transmission of this publication
may be made without written permission.
No paragraph of this publication may be reproduced,
copied or transmitted save with the written permission of the publisher,
or in accordance with the provisions
of the Copyright Act 1956 (as amended).

Any person who commits any unauthorized act in relation to
this publication may be liable to criminal
prosecution and civil claims for damage.

A CIP catalog record for this title is
available from the British Library.

ISBN: 978-1-80439-792-3

This is a work of fiction.
Names, characters, places and incidents originate from the writer's
imagination. Any resemblance to actual persons, living or dead, is
purely coincidental.

First Published in 2024

Olympia Publishers
Tallis House
2 Tallis Street
London
EC4Y 0AB

Printed in Great Britain

Dear Mohammed Al Ajlouni,
Malala Yousafzai,
Greta Thunberg,
You are as much my children as my Oday and Maryam.
So, I ask you to forgive my motherly eyes,
for they managed to weigh on them but failed to walk with you.

The Scenic Route

Her neighbors spoke of a movement rising in a faraway land. "What do they want?" she asked.

"Equality, for a woman to be treated as an equal to a man," someone explained. She nodded her head politely, pretending to understand, what for the life of her, she did not. As far as Oyoun Almaha was aware, women were superior to men, who, like everything else, were created to serve her.

Safflower and carmine were created to color her lips red, and men were created to find those and transform them into an applicable powder. Chickens were created to give her child-bearing muscles strength, and men to breed, slaughter, and skin that chicken for her. Oranges to give her a glow, and men to negotiate with Morocco and Spain so that they could fetch her the sweetest pick. Gold was her favorite embellishment, and it was a man's job to melt and remold that gold, presenting her with the most beautiful jewelry.

She believed every woman was granted a superpower: her charm. And with that power comes the responsibility to manipulate men to achieve their highest potential.

Oyoun Almaha looked out her window with scrutinizing eyes; the builder across the street took the arch leading to the foyer a meter higher and would not have stopped until he got that shy, satisfied smile from her. He knocked down and rebuilt the pillars three times before he had her approving nod. The man pushing the vegetable cart checked his tomatoes twenty times before stepping into her alley. God forbid she picks one and lets out a disappointed '*tsss.*' The last time her hand put back a rotten tomato, he could not fathom the idea of parting with something she had touched; he lovingly ate it, then tossed and turned in pain all night.

Her husband, the clothier, spent all day unrolling and rolling yards of fabric in front of difficult-to-please customers. After all the stores were closed, and he watched the last person leave the marketplace, he carried his heavy collection over his back and up the stairs to lock it in a safe storage room. Exhausted yet very determined, he begged for a ride west to buy Oyoun Almaha some flour from the only grinder she trusted. From there, he caught another ride east for cumin because she did not approve of all the other spice stalls. He came back, walked an extra ten meters to his house, and greeted her with a warm smile and a compliment. She spread a display of food in front of him, which he did not touch until she had the first bite.

All was good in the world of man and woman until one day a young lady thought her time and charm were too precious to be wasted on a boy. So, she seduced an older, well-established man who was also a father and someone else's husband. That did not stop her, well, because bending the rules a little never killed anyone. By some miracle, that man believed he had something to do with this transaction, and that it was he who had replaced his older, unfulfilling wife with a younger woman. For many years, men danced a weary dance around this thought until more women convinced them it was possible.

Oyoun Almaha was introduced to this idea of replaceable wives not by her dreamy husband, who could not keep his eyes or mind off her, but by me, her own daughter. The day I refused to marry Kareem, the eldest son of a wealthy family and a respectful lawyer himself. I chose to go to college instead. I wish I had the option of doing both, but in my community, a wife had more important things to attend to. "I need to be able to take care of myself, incase my husband leaves me for a younger woman," I said to my mother.

"By the time you graduate college, you will be too old, and no one will want to marry you, let alone leave you," she snapped at me.

"Mama, an education is just as important as starting a family."

"An education! There was a time when people traveled seas, valleys, and mountains in search of knowledge. They found that knowledge in the wisdom of hakeems and sages. In addition to the profound information these teachers shared with them, they learned many lessons along the way from nature itself, and some from the common man, woman, or child they conversed or ate with. They came out of that journey with something to say that the world did not already know. Today they lock hundreds of children in rooms, repeatedly force them to memorize information that has been sitting unquestioned in books for years. Then, they hand them another piece of paper with their names, telling them that they now know all they need to know, and a number deeming their intelligence to a mere percentage. If you had said to me that you had an unexplainable desire to unravel one of the universe's secrets, I would have sent you away myself. But this, wasting your life for a piece of paper to label you capable of work just because you are worried a man like Kareem would marry you, then leave you for a younger woman, I don't understand."

I tried to defend myself, but Oyoun Almaha raised her right hand and turned her face the other way, hiding her trembling lips.

As was customary, my mother had three days before she was obliged to give the boy's family an official answer. She spent two and a half of those days rocking her head back and forth in her palms, looking at the sky and then at me for a sign that I had a change of heart. Sometimes I believe she was more worried about what she was going to say to Kareem's mother than me actually missing out on a good opportunity. I heard her practice her speech, "My daughter has lost her mind. She will never find a better man than Kareem," she paused, and then answered herself, "You are her mother! Talk some sense into her."

Somewhere in the middle of the third day, just as I started to doubt my resolution and believe I was pushing it too far, and that I might cause my mother to go mad, her eyes fell on my younger sister, Nargis.

I was nothing like my mother, but Nargis looked and behaved exactly like her. I woke up in the morning, pulled my hair back in a ponytail, threw a blanket over my bed, and then rushed to get ready for school. Nargis woke up with a big smile, fluffed her hair, hummed a song, and spent at least five minutes arranging decorative cushions on her pretty bed. I rushed through chores so I could do my homework; she used cooking and cleaning as an excuse to escape from her books. I spent my evenings biting my nails and solving math problems while she scrubbed her hands with sugar and olive oil and painted her nails pink.

Oyoun Almaha took a moment to carefully observe Nargis, who strolled around the house with her chin pointing up high, her heart open to the heavens, and her long receptive arms welcoming all the world had to offer. There was nothing shy about her smile. Her gaze had more surrender than scrutiny, and the men circling around her did not work hard for her approval.

They lazily drooled about, waiting for her to slip so they could have her.

While Nargis twirled around to old romantic songs, my mother washed up, laid out her prayer mat, and fell to the ground "Forgive me, ya Allah, for doubting your ways," she cried with a big smile, realizing that God had blessed us with Kareem, not for me, but to protect my all-grown-up sister's sanctity. She put on a nice gown, hurried to the patisserie down the street, bought a fresh tray of *baklava,* and then knocked on Kareem's mother's door. She sat in front of her, a little embarrassed and somewhat excited. "Om Kareem, you are like a sister to me. No! No, you are more than a sister. That is why I am comfortable speaking to you transparently from the heart. I love Kareem deeply and cannot think of a better family to give my daughter to, but the thing is…" she paused to catch her breath and then continued, "Salma wants to go to college. You know children nowadays; they don't care about our traditions and want to play every game women in the west are playing."

My mother noticed a frown on Kareem's mother's face; she saw how she looked at the tray of celebratory sweets in confusion and quickly blurted out, "Please, accept my younger daughter, Nargis. I promise she will make a better wife for your son."

"But isn't Nargis too young?" The boy's mother asked.

"She is seventeen, knows everything there is to know about keeping a house, and is ready for marriage. You've seen her."

Kareem's mother was flattered. Nargis was, after all, a much prettier bride for her son.

There was a big engagement party with lots of food, flowers, music, and dancing. But all I could think about were the whispers, "Poor, Salma! He chose her younger sister over her." I managed to hold myself together, and stay composed through the evening, and until I washed and put away the last glass, then ran to my father's arms. I told him what everyone was saying and cried. He held my cheeks in his hands. "Do you want to marry Kareem? Or do you want to pursue your independence?" he firmly asked me.

"I want my independence." I wiped my tears as I answered.

"Then do not let what they say distract you. A voice inside you demanded your attention and pushed you far enough to stand up to your mother. Now see that you tend to that voice, even if things get a little ugly. In this journey of life, we can't always choose the scenic route."

Nargis jumped onto my bed, lay next to me, and wrote a letter to Kareem about how she was plagued with his love, willing to dissolve in his shadow, become anything he wants her to be, and crumble in his arms.

We spent a whole week scrubbing, waxing, and soaking my baby sister in milk for Kareem. On the day of the wedding, my mother locked all my cousins and friends out. No one, except her and I, were allowed to see the bride until she was ready. When Oyoun Almaha failed to control her shaking hands, she passed me the powder pad and snapped, "Apply it evenly." Nargis did not object to anything I did to her. It did not matter if I overdid it with the powder, or if the lipstick I smudged on her cheeks was too red. She knew her beauty was breathtaking and nothing could change that. Our female relatives and friends gathered in our living room and received the women from Kareem's family. The elders sang some happy songs, welcoming the guests, then some sad words, describing how every corner of the house would long for their child's giggles once she had left for her new life. After dinner, the women covered up and made way for the groom. He marched in and straight to my mother's room, where Nargis was waiting. He opened the door, stood next to her. She slipped her hand in the gap through his bent elbow, and our guests caught a glimpse of the bride as she walked out and into her husband's car. The rest of us squeezed into different cars and followed them through town, honking and clapping all the way to Kareem's house. Nargis stepped out, looking like an angel in her white satin dress and tulle veil. She smiled as her eyes victoriously took in the neighborhood. We sat her down on the edge of a bed that was covered in rose petals in a room suffocated with burning incense, and left.

The next morning, my mother and I rushed to her house. I huddled against a group of women in a tiny corridor. Nargis stepped out of her room, her hair wet and her eyes…

Those traumatized eyes still haunt me. They blame me for dooming my sister to what should have been my fate.

"Are you okay?" I asked her.

"He did not look into my eyes, not even once! We were together all night. Not once did he look into my eyes," she managed to say to me before her mother-in-law and our mother stepped out of the bedroom, celebrating the bloody evidence of my sister's innocence. The aunties let out *ulullies,* and kissed her head for making them proud. They instantly snapped her out of her terror and laid out a list of responsibilities she had to perform to keep her husband satisfied and her home intact.

I passed by her house every other day, mostly out of guilt. I saw her chipped nails, her cracked heels, and that broken strand of hair. I saw the bruise on her arm when I accidentally walked in on her while she was changing. I knew my mother saw it too. We both saw our Nargis's eyes lose victory and disappointment; for a while, they seemed like they were searching, waiting for something. Then, they were just empty. She never complained, and always smiled when she came to visit, or when Kareem walked through the door. She smiled when her first, then second son did something to grab her attention, but her lifeless eyes never looked directly at any of us. If I had not known better, I would have thought she was blind.

One afternoon, Kareem came home, while she was dragging out a heavy black garbage bag and caught their elderly neighbor staring at her ankles.

"He looked into my eyes for the very first time today," she told me.

"Finally, it took him five years; Why aren't you happy?" I asked teasingly.

"He stared straight into my eyes for five whole minutes to see if I was guilty of seducing our old neighbor." She bit her lip and banged the table.

All I could think about was how dry her eyes were.

In some twisted way to show the neighbor his place, Kareem offered Ghalib, the man's nineteen-year-old son, a ridiculous amount of money to take out their garbage. Kareem knew the young man was saving up to buy himself a laptop and would not refuse an opportunity to earn something extra. What he did not know is that; Ghalib had been in love with Nargis ever since he saw her step out of the car on her wedding day. He was playing football with his friends when she appeared out of nowhere and took hold of his heart. The old neighbor was oblivious to the reason behind this job offer, and like any wise father was happy, his son did not allow his pride to come in the way of an honest earning. Ghalib tried plenty but failed to convince his mind that it was sinful to fantasize about another man's wife. Besides, he did not find Kareem to be worthy of much respect, and to add to that, he could not help but notice how Kareem was mistreating his Nargis.

Ghalib swung in and out of the house like a ghost for months. Then he saw her, the delicate princess of his dreams, struggling to open a ladder. He grabbed a hold of it. She nervously let go and took a few steps back. "What do you need to do?" He asked.

"I want to dust the chandelier."

"Give it to me. I will do it." He reached his hand out for her to hand him a cloth she was holding.

"No! I will do it."

"Fine, I will hold the ladder for you."

She nervously looked toward the door, and he got that she was afraid her husband could come home any minute and misunderstand. "I will be outside. Open the door when you are done. I will come and put the ladder away." He stepped out until she let him back in again. Ghalib put the ladder away and left. He gradually started to help out with more. A leaking faucet, a pickle jar, the boys' remote-controlled car, and hanging paintings that had been lying on the living room floor for years.

He came across Nargis at the park one day, a book tucked under her armpit, a different toy, and a snack in each hand, juggling between both boys. "Come, let's play some football." He pulled them away from her. She took a deep breath and looked at him with a smile. He winked and pointed his chin at her book. She sat back and started to read. A few minutes later, he caught her eyes escaping the book, and looking at a *kebab* stand nearby. He slipped away from the boys and sat on a bench next to hers. "Do you want a sandwich?" he asked.

"I already ate lunch, thank you," she answered without looking at him.

"But do you want a sandwich now?"

"Boys, do you want a sandwich?" she called out.

"No, Mama," the eldest answered.

"Nargis, do you want a sandwich?" Ghalib asked more firmly.

She did not answer. He bought two sandwiches and watched her gobble them up, with tears rolling down her cheeks.

At the end of the month, he walked into the house, grabbed a garbage bag, and looked for his money on the counter where he usually found it. He thought about leaving as he already had a little more than what he needed to buy a laptop. But then he decided to find Nargis and ask her why Kareem did not leave him his money where he was supposed to.

Ghalib found Nargis lying upside down on a sofa, her long curls wildly dangling on the floor, her naked legs up in the air, and her hands holding his money against her stomach. She swung to her feet, her red dress followed. She stood close to him, gently stroking his face with the back of her fingers, his money still in that same hand. Her eyes locked into his. He grabbed her hand, folded her fingers around the money, fell to his knees, and kissed the floor next to her foot.

"What are you doing?" She jumped back.

"Kissing the dust that touched your feet," he smiled and walked away backward.

Ghalib went to the electronics store, stared at the laptop he had dreamed about for months, and bought a phone for Nargis. They spent hours talking to each other, lurking in an alternate reality where she was not someone's wife or mother, where she was nothing but a beautiful young woman worthy of all the love in the world.

One rainy night, while Kareem was out with a friend, Nargis called Ghalib and said, "I cannot do this any more. I cannot display in front of God what I am afraid people would find out.

Fear is also a form of worship, reserved after all, only for the almighty." She hung up and switched her phone off.

Ghalib sat on his front step for days, hoping he could catch her when she eventually walked out. Before that happened, Kareem pulled over in his car, rolled his window down, and called out, "Hey, Ghalib! Come help me with these boxes." He opened the trunk and went inside, leaving Ghalib with three heavy boxes.

Ghalib picked up a box and followed Kareem inside. He saw Nargis, too nervous to notice him standing there; she rushed between the stove and putting her husband's keys in a bowl near the front entrance, where he liked to find them. Kareem sat on the sofa, his head resting back, and eyes closed. She squatted in front of him, he placed his foot on her knee, and she untied his lace. Ghalib dropped the box, shattering everything inside. Startled, Nargis fell back. Without moving his head, Kareem yelled, "You idiot, you will have to pay for the glasses you broke."

Ghalib grabbed Nargis by the shoulders and lifted her off the ground.

"How dare you touch my wife?" Kareem jumped to his feet and raised a hand to hit Ghalib, but the look in the young man's eyes scared him.

"Take me away from here," Nargis said, clinging on to Ghalib's arm. They took the children out of their room and left Kareem standing there.

We were still trying to understand what had happened when Kareem came pounding at our door. "Are you just going to stand there while she leaves me for that boy? Or will you talk some sense into her?" He screamed at my father.

"There was a week between the day you asked for my

daughter's hand and the day I placed it in yours. Do you know how many times I suffocated myself that week? How many inner voices I silenced, convincing myself you were worthy of the most precious thing in the world? Do you know I wished I was dead every time she came to visit, and I could clearly see how unhappy she was but could not bring myself to ask? How I wished she would complain just once, so I could find you and rip your heart out. Now, leave before I forget you are the father of my grandchildren, and I lose my mind."

Oyoun Almaha dragged Nargis into her room and pushed her on to the bed. "Shut the door," she yelled at me. I stepped inside and closed the door. "What has gotten into you?" she mumbled, like she was afraid someone would hear.

"What if Kareem had cheated on you?" she asked Nargis.

"What if Kareem had cheated on me? Ha! The whole world would have asked me what I was doing wrong, told me to dress better, to cook more, to swallow my pride, humiliate myself a little more, and try harder to make him a happier man. You would have told me to look the other way. Pretend I did not know, and not wreck my house over a silly mistake. You would have told me to think of my children and forgive him."

"What can that boy give you that your husband won't?" she lost her temper and yelled now.

"Respect, Mama! He respects me. Maybe the question you should ask is: what can Kareem take from me that Ghalib will not? And the answer is that we give them all we have. The only difference is that one man's whore can be another's goddess," Nargis answered with a condescending smile that shut us all up.

Ghalib hovered around our house for three months, waiting for Nargis to complete her *Iddah,* and be allowed to marry again.
– "*A divorced woman is required to wait out an Iddah of three*

months, to rule out a pregnancy, or reconcile before the marriage is legally terminated."

Two days before Nargis's *Iddah* finally came to an end, my mother turned our living room into a beauty parlor. She called in someone to scrub Nargis and bathe her in milk and rose water. Treat and blow dry her hair, paint her nails, and massage her feet.

While we were trying to wash away all evidence of Kareem, a messenger from his office knocked on our door with a letter. Oyoun Almaha opened it. "Kareem is threatening that if Nargis doesn't return to him, he will take the boys away and never allow her to see them," she told me as she ripped the paper to pieces. I followed her out and into a taxi that took us to my father's shop. Baba was too busy serving customers to ask what we were doing there. She grabbed the biggest pair of scissors she could find and stomped toward Kareem's house. "Mama," I begged her to stop, but she was in a trance. She banged on his door.

"If you ever use your children to manipulate my child again, I will kill them, and after you have buried them, I will kill you." She pointed the scissors in his face, and then turned to me with a look that said, "Your sister has been through enough pain, and we will do whatever it takes to make sure she goes through no more."

From then on, no grandparent, uncle, aunt, cousin, or friend was allowed anywhere near her, until one of us had first filtered the entire conversation they intended to have with her. And even then, we carefully monitored them and were not one bit reluctant to cut their visit short and show them the way out.

Ghalib begged his parents to accompany him to ask for Nargis's hand, but they brushed off his request like it was child's play. So, he came to see my mother alone. "Ghalib, go get yourself a proper job and rent a house worthy of my daughter, then come and ask for her." I watched Oyoun Almaha making these demands and wished our parents demanded the men who asked for us were just as much mentally and emotionally prepared as they were financially.

Nargis and Ghalib got married four years later and were blessed with a baby girl. The boys spend weekdays with their mother and go see Kareem on the weekends. Now, Nargis looks into our eyes as she tells us a joke and laughs until her eyes tear up. She runs to Ghalib's arms when he walks through the door and tells him about her day. She sings to her children and dances at weddings until she loses her breath.

I married Zayn, a liberal man who respected my choice to pursue a career. The first time we met was in an elevator at a business tower downtown. He looked right at me and said, "Hello." I nodded with a smile and tried my best to avoid looking in his direction. He found me waiting for a taxi outside and asked if I needed a ride.

"No, thank you," I answered, my eyes nervously glued to my phone.

"Take my number; it could take a taxi forever to get here. You might need me to come back for you," he said. I took his number because it was a little past dark and I was not used to being in that part of town. Having someone to call seemed like a good idea. Instead of leaving, he stood there with a bemused smirk on his face until my taxi arrived. He opened the door for me and told me to call him when I got home. "I will assume something bad happened to you if you don't. I will call the police and demand they check every taxi." I obediently called him to let him know I made it home safely.

As a child, Zayn accompanied his father on the fields. He sat on a pile of hay, or a rock, and watched the farmer's bare feet sink into paddies while he respectfully grazed the soil. He watched his strong, sweaty father pray to God with desperation, and whisper to the seeds with a friendly authority, before allowing them to slip out of his fingers into the dirt, where he believed he too would one day end up resting.

First thing in the morning, his father would gaze into the sky and explain to Zayn how some sunshines are good and others not so much. How some rains are meant to be met with open arms, contained and made use of, while others we watch through a window and ignore as they disappear into the mud. Some storms clear the heavy air from lingering diseases, and others are pointless.

Come harvest time, he greeted the field "*Asalam Alaikum*," before entering his right foot first, bowed his head, thanked the plants, and asked them for permission before picking their offerings. He never weighed or counted his earnings and always slept like a fulfilled man.

The farmer did not take his son down to the fields in an attempt to teach him secrets of the trade, so one day he could become a farmer just like him. He took him out there to teach him what they did not teach him at school: that a man's body is equipped with enough strength and perseverance to face any hardship. He wanted to teach him that there would always be something out of his control. He wanted to teach him to respect everything, small and big.

Zayn grew up, left the village, and lived in executive towers and suits. His father continued to work, despite his wife's bitter warnings, "I am not going to take care of you if you fall and break a hip." He leaned on his walking stick and hired a young man who carefully followed his every instruction until one day he could no longer find his voice, and soon his lungs gave up on him.

Without delay, Zayn claimed his inheritance hired a few peasants to manage the land, and came back every month to collect his earnings. He kissed his mother's hand, slipped some cash in it, and yelled out to the closest employee, "Take care of my mother. Make sure she has everything she needs." His mother stood at the door and watched him hop into his jeep. She raised her hand with a prayer, "May Allah protect you and bless you wherever you go."

It is Tuesday, September the twentieth, 2022. I get into my car, run the air-conditioner, ask Siri to play *The Start the Day Right* playlist, drive closer to the gate, and wait for my teenage kids to come out. Mo's fist was clenched, his face red. He shoved his sister with his shoulder. "I told you I did not see you," Elena tried to defend herself.

"How could you not see me? You shut the door in my face on purpose!" He muttered under his breath because he was afraid I would yell at him, and oh God, did I want to.

This was not the first time my kids followed me out with a fight after I left them alone for two minutes. Just two minutes, to bring the car closer so they would not have to walk a few extra steps or wait for the car to cool down. It usually took me another minute to snap and remind them of all the things their father and I did so they would be happy, and how hurtful it was that they were not. I would go on about the ripple effect and how they were spreading negativity. How one of them needed to be the bigger person and not engage when the other was being unreasonable.

This time, I reminded myself of a video on parenting I had watched earlier that week. I reminded myself how yelling at my children could scar them forever and tried something different. I took a deep breath and counted to ten, then said, "Look, it's a monkey!" I slowed down a little and pretended to be looking at a monkey. We lived in a city where there were hardly any trees, let alone wild monkeys.

"Where, Mama?" My thirteen-year-old Elena asked with excitement.

"There, it was jumping on the roof of that white building." I pointed and pulled over. I could see Mo's fist and forehead relax a little. About thirty seconds later, they gave up on my imaginary monkey, pulled out their phones, and watched videos about squirrels and cats.

I looked at them and an image from my past presented itself. My mother hiding her face behind a raised hand, just like I could see her quivering lips behind that hand, behind my children's phones. I saw Mo's suppressed anger, and Elena forcefully sucking up her tears.

What was happening? Why did my son feel compelled to demand respect from his younger sister? I wonder how it would have gone if I had allowed their argument to play out. I wonder if we have taken this whole women's empowerment scene a little too far. When my son looks at his sister, does he even see how fragile and small she is? Does he have an instinct to protect her? Or does he see a superhero capable of fighting next to Superman? A villainess who can take a shove or blow to the stomach and hop right back up on her feet? When he shoved her, was he the least bit worried she might fall on the pavement and hurt herself? Would he never hurt her or any other woman if he wasn't scared that I would ground him or take his phone away?

What about Elena? Does she know it is okay to depend on a man? In our tireless attempts to make her strong, have we deprived her of the right to feel protected, to dream of being swept off her feet? Does she believe there are men she could trust and who won't let her down?

I dropped my children off at school and headed to my office. Members of the board gathered in a meeting room to congratulate me on the success of my marketing campaign. I had spent the last year and a half putting together the perfect combination of colors, images, music, and words to manipulate the consumer's mind and double our sales. I rushed out of the room, struggling to hold back tears of joy, and dialed my husband. Somewhat because a husband is the first person you share news of making partner with, and somewhat because I wanted to rub my success in that ever-doubting man's face, who always belittled my competence.

When he did not answer, I convinced myself we would celebrate over dinner, which I served on our special occasion dishes with some candles and non-alcoholic wine. He was on a phone call when he walked in and finished eating while I was still in the kitchen heating bread. He covered the bottom part of his phone and said, "I saved you this. It's really good," tilting his head toward half a *samosa*. I swallowed whatever I could and cleaned up, while he changed and watched a football match on T.V. I put the last glass back where it belongs and fell to the kitchen floor. If I walked in there and interrupted his game to share my good news or concerns about our children, he would call me a *nikadiah* – A grouch who ruins one's good mood – my wife is a *nikadiah,* was also the most acceptable excuse for a man to have an affair or marry a second, less *nikadiah,* who would respect his need to unwind after a long day at work. However, if I walked in there in my sexy red lingerie, his game would not be as important.

How did I get here? I upset my mother and sacrificed my sister for a life independent from a Kareem, and here I was, my very happiness depending on a Zayn. How did I allow myself to get distracted? How many imaginary monkeys did I follow?

Do not get me wrong, I love my husband very much. I love him for giving me a home. I hate that only the walls know my most intimate secrets. I love my husband for always making sure I'm safe. I hate him for tearing down my confidence. I love him for giving me children. I hate that his absence makes him a hard-working hero, while my work only means I wasn't there to catch them when they stumbled on their first step or answer when they spoke their first "Mama". I loved my husband for being a good father to our kids; I hated him for believing that was enough to make him a good husband. My husband never forgot an anniversary or birthday and always showered me with the most valuable gifts. I love him for that. I hate all the things I was guilted into doing in return. I loved him for being considerate with my family and hated him for neglecting his own. I loved how brave he was with business and hated how he gambled with my children's financial security. I loved how focused he was on his goals. I hated how invisible that made me. I loved my husband because I wanted to be in love, and he was my husband.

I sat there on my kitchen floor and stared at the ceiling. The bright fluorescent lights hurt my eyes as I asked my dead father, "Now what, Baba? Do I choose the scenic route, or do I walk the shabby alleys, through the smelly sewers, and unclog my drains before I drown in my own filth?"

The Root of All Suffering Is Deliberate Ignorance

On the first night of Muharram, the beginning of a new year on the Hijri calendar, my mother gave my sister and me our annual haircut. She sat me on a stool, tied a plastic table cover around my neck, sprayed my hair with water, and combed it backward, then cut no more than half an inch off the end. I was about to get up and give Nargis her turn when my mother started to play with my hair. She twisted and turned it in a bun, lifted it high on my head, let it down, then did it a little looser. "We will put your hair up on your wedding, and I will have a lace veil with heavy work made for you. It will suit your face," she said.

"Don't be silly, Mama, I'm not even engaged yet," I said with a forced smile and a twist in my stomach. Just that morning, our neighbor had come over and whispered to my mother about how her husband did not come home all night again.

"Why do you tolerate him?" Oyoun Almaha asked with a harsh tone.

"What other choice do I have?" She broke down. I looked at my mother and waited for her to give the woman an answer, but she had none.

That question rang in my ears for days. What *choice did she have? Where would she go with her five children? And how could she leave them with a man who was never home?* Then my eyes fell on a magazine displayed on a shelf at the marketplace. It had a rather unusual cover. My mother was haggling with the storekeeper over rice, so I had plenty of time to hold it in my hand and study it. On the cover was a woman who looked nothing like any woman I had ever seen before. She stared at me with a fierce glare; she had short hair, wore a black suit, white shirt, black high heels, and sat on an office chair, her elbow resting on her wide-open legs in a manner only a man would be daring enough to carry.

I did not know who she was, so I invented a different story about her every day. One day she was an architect who designed skyscrapers, scribbled on blueprints, and yelled at younger men and women for suggesting poor ideas. She had an office on the top floor of one of her buildings, where she stood and stared out the window at the world she conquered. Or she could have owned her own jewelry brand. She had a big walk-in safe in the basement of her building, where she stored a selection of only the purest stones. She did morning rounds between workstations and told her designers to make those earrings bigger, and that necklace shorter. She was interviewed by this magazine for her outstanding ability to conquer the market. She also could have been in the food business and somehow managed to control prices of chicken and tomato, so the poor enjoyed as many meals as the wealthy.

Whoever she was, I wanted to be her, and not the woman who had no other choice. I followed my father's instructions and allowed nothing to distract me. Ten years later, I was not the woman on the magazine cover. I was something bigger; I was the person who created women like her.

A bank launching a new product was one of my clients at the agency I worked for. The product was a low-interest loan that would presumably help an individual attain his dream life. I led our art director, Waheeb, and a team of creatives, and spent months back and forth between them and the client until we had an approved concept for the campaign. Success no longer required long years of hard work; with the help of our bank, even a young family could afford a big house and a convertible.

We figured that casting a fresh set of talent who were not recognized models or actors would make our story more credible. We flew a male model in from Turkey; our female was a local whose headshots had everyone in the office stunned. She came in wearing an ivory kaftan, flip-flops, and her long curly hair looked like it had not been washed in days, but we were trained to see beyond that. To compensate for her shyness, she held a five-year-old son in her hand that was not one bit shy of us or the camera. Lara and her boy were exactly what we needed to complete an image that matched our story boards. Our location of choice was a mansion on the beach, an hour and a half drive from the city, so the sensible thing to do was to move the entire crew out there for a week.

Since Lara and I were the only women, we were offered to share the master bedroom, while Waheeb and the male model took a smaller bedroom each. The rest of the crew just spread out through the house.

Lara's son, Adam, excitedly bounced all over the big bed. She nervously straightened the covers and scolded him. "It's okay, you guys take the bed. I will sleep on the couch," I stopped her.

"Don't be silly. It is big enough for all of us," she said joyfully.

"You remind me of my little sister, Nargis." I smiled.

"I am an only child. I always wished I had an older sister to take care of me," all the joy in her voice disappeared.

As directed by Waheeb, everyone was up by three a.m., so

we could be ready and catch the early sunrise light. We then took a break until an hour before sunset, so we could catch our models under that light.

Waheeb and I had lunch by the pool and were staring at our laptops when Lara brought little Adam down for a swim. Waheeb slammed his laptop shut and jumped in the water. He played with the boy, while not so subtly checking Lara out. He came back to the table, and when she was done drying up, her son waved at her to join us. She looked at me and waited until I told her it was okay.

"I'm Waheeb," he offered her a handshake.

"Lara," she giggled and played along.

"Nice to meet you, Lara. What do you do?"

"I am a model. What do you do?"

"I am an art director. I have an eye for beauty, and when I see something beautiful, I have a tendency to capture it," he said, gazing right into her eyes. She shook her head and smiled shyly.

"So, Lara, why did you choose to become a model?" he asked.

Lara fell silent, sent Adam away to play, and then answered, "It was the easiest way for me to get a divorce."

"So, who wants coffee?" Waheeb, not so happy with where the conversation was heading, changed the subject.

Waheeb was a loud, charismatic personality, who managed to fill any space he walked in to and turn it into a party. He was in his late forties, divorced twice, and survived ugly battles to be able to spend some time with his three children. Now, he was fighting against time. Refusing to age, he ate, drank, and smoked like a self-destructive twenty-year-old. I never engaged in his drama and made it clear on the first day I met him that we shall never discuss anything that fell out of the scope of work. So, even then and there, I showed no interest in his personal conversation with our model. I could tell from the way Lara empathetically looked at him, patiently waiting for him to open up, that she saw beyond his happy facade. She saw his pain, his defeat, and his loneliness. I thought perhaps it was her motherly instinct that instigated a need to nurture him.

Throughout the day, Waheeb would ask Lara how she was doing, whether he could get her anything, whether she had eaten. He fetched her a new glass of juice every few hours and made sure she had the herbal tea she liked in the evening. He showered Adam with love and spent hours playing with him. There was something unsettling about his kindness. It reminded me of the wicked woman from Hansel and Gretel's house made of sweets, but I said nothing and watched Lara grow more and more fascinated by him. One evening after Adam fell asleep, we decided to go sit outside by the beach. It wasn't long before Waheeb found us and sat right next to her. He whispered in her ear and showed her something on his phone. I stepped away to avoid the awkwardness, then suddenly heard her lash out, "I don't know. I've been married my whole adult life. I only did what married people do." I followed her as she ran back to our room. I expected her to slam the door, but once inside, she was overcome by a strange calm. She quietly closed the door, changed, and slipped into bed.

The next day, Waheeb shooed her off the sets. "We don't need you today. We are going to work on the shots you are not a part of." She obediently nodded and wandered around us like a lost kitten, then came back and asked Waheeb if he wanted her to make him some coffee. He dismissed her twice, and a few hours later called out to her, "Lara, be a doll and fetch me a bottle of water." She brought him one, and he finally gave her a smile.

When he called her that evening, she must have thought it no longer made sense to hide their relationship from me, so she openly spoke to him. I could hear every word he said through her phone, "Lara, I was just sharing my thoughts with you. We may never be together or do any of those things. It does not matter. I like you and just want to get to know you better."

She humored him until he asked her, "If you could come to my room right now, what would you do?"

"I am tired, Waheeb, I should sleep, or my eyes will look bad tomorrow."

"Nothing we cannot retouch," he said. She looked in my direction. I pretended to be sleeping.

"See you tomorrow, bye," she said with a fake laugh and hung up.

Somewhere around the middle of the week, we all gathered in an empty reception hall to review what we had accomplished so far. Waheeb stood in the center of the room and, in a very serious tone, gave our models and technical team some crucial feedback. He looked at me and instructed me on what I needed to communicate with the client, and then shouted out, "Cheer up, everyone. We're doing great."

I paced around a corner, on the phone with our client, ignoring half of Waheeb's instructions and agreeing with everything the client had to say. When I turned around, I saw Adam had fallen asleep on a pile of jackets everyone else had left, and Waheeb was saying something to Lara that was clearly upsetting her. I told my client I had to call her back and quickly went closer to them. "Lara, I swear it is not like that. I just want to know everything about you," he told her once again.

"You want to know everything about me? Fine, listen." She crawled away from him and curled into herself. I froze in my place and listened too.

"My father was the eldest male in our big family, so all our relatives, close and distant, often visited to pay respect. They were never allowed to leave without a meal, which meant my mother was always busy in the kitchen preparing something or the other. At some point, an uncle would take me upstairs to give me candy. He spread out across the table more candy than I was allowed or perhaps able to eat and asked me to show him if I could count them all, and if I could name all their colors. All I could think about was which one I wanted to eat first. I did not wonder why we had to be alone upstairs, or why I had to be so close to him. I did not like it, but I also did not like how he held me or kissed my cheek when I greeted him. When I tried to avoid that, my father yelled at me for misbehaving, so I did not misbehave when we were upstairs. Occasionally, an elder cousin offered to play hide and seek. All my six-year-old brain heard was *play*. I did not know who we were hiding from, or why his hand had to be where it was. My mother found us eventually; she blamed me and accused me of provoking him. Now, she kept an eye on me. She yelled at me for smiling at the driver, standing by the window, or answering the door.

When I turned sixteen, I met Zakaria on my way back from school. Instead of believing I was filthy, Zakaria treated me like I was sacred. He walked tall behind me in the alleys, so all the men looked away. When he bought me chocolates, he stood two feet away and watched me eat. He went with me to the market and made sure no one addressed me directly and spoke to him instead. He refused to touch me until we were married, and when he asked my father for my hand, my father refused because he did not have a college degree, which meant he could not give me a proper home.

I was in the living room one afternoon studying when a pinch in my gut forced me to look up. My uncle stood by the door; he did not have any candy and stood as far away from me as possible. *"I have leukemia. I will not survive. I need you to forgive me,"* he said.

"Ask again," I said.

"Please, please, forgive me," he begged.

"Not here. There," I pointed at the sky, *"in front of everyone and God, on judgment day."* He left, but I kept staring at that door, then later in the night at my bedroom door. I turned off the lights, and I heard him breathing down my neck. I turned on the lights; the furniture shamed me. I snuck downstairs and out of the house. I enjoyed the quiet dark alley until the silence was interrupted with an intoxicated laughter. I found our neighborhood boys sitting on the pavement, snatched a joint out of one's hand, and sat with them. He told me how pretty I was, and I led him to believe that one day he would have his way with me. A few months later, he threatened to stop supplying me if I did not keep my end of the bargain. I found another gullible boy who fought with his childhood friend, and gave me what I wanted for a little longer.

My father found me a suitor. My cousin, not the one who played with me, but my good cousin Jameel. He was a doctor, who rented me a nice home and brought me gifts every time he came for a visit. On my wedding night, my father held me by the shoulders and told me that, with the right attitude, a woman could have any man under her thumb. Jameel knew nothing about my ugly past and treated me like a queen right until we entered the bedroom. There, after kissing me, he would pull my hair, call me names, tell me to call myself those names, and say, "You're mine, say you're my whore." Then, after he was done hurting me, he would laugh like someone had given him a flattering compliment and ask me if I enjoyed myself. I did not know if that was something I was meant to enjoy. All anyone had ever told me about what happened between a husband and wife was that if I refused him his rights, Allah would bestow a *La'anah – a curse expelling me forever from his mercy* – on me. I'm sure Jameel did not learn his bedroom manners from his father, either. Then one day, we were introduced to movies, uncensored romantic novels, and the internet, and once I knew what I knew, I could not pretend I did not.

It was impossible for me to tell my parents that I wanted a divorce. They would ask why, and what would I say? So, I hid in the bathroom and cried for hours every morning until God showed me a way out. A lady approached me while I was buying spices. She told me I had a beautiful smile and asked if I could model for her Kaftan store. Just a few pictures to display in a catalog. I was certain Jameel would never allow me to do anything like that, and there was no way on earth he would stay married to me if I did it without his permission. So, I went to her store the next morning and posed in all the kaftans she wanted. Jameel divorced me and made it clear he did not want anything to do with me or my son, and there was no way in hell I would take my child to live at my parent's house where I grew up. The kind owner of the kaftan store lent me some money for rent, which I am working to pay back.

Waheeb pulled her closer to him and told her everything was going to be okay. She broke down in his arms and cried until she laughed.

Watching Lara pose for the camera the next day was the most beautiful thing. She was so confident and comfortable; she gave us the most captivating images.

Waheeb was nice to her up until our last night at the resort when he gave her an ultimatum. She either had to go see him in his room that night or delete his number. Lara packed her stuff, and as she zipped her suitcase closed, she said to me, "You know what I wish?"

"What?" I asked.

"I wish I could tell my father he was wrong... that a woman's attitude is not what keeps a man under her thumb," she said, her lips melting into a disappointed smile.

"You don't have to do anything you don't want to," I said to her.

"I don't know what I want or don't want. I wanted candy; does that mean I wanted my filthy uncle all over me? I wanted to play; I was lonely and bored. Does that mean I wanted to provoke my cousin? I wanted to get high so I could fall asleep without worrying someone would come into my room. I wanted to get high enough to forget that look my mother had on her face. Does that mean I also wanted to mislead those poor boys? I wanted a house with doors I could lock. Does that mean I also wanted to be my husband's whore? I wanted someone to like me and care for my son. I was tired of trying to win, and always failing. I was tired of shielding myself and wanted to surrender; to let go and submit to someone. Does that also mean I wanted to succumb to Waheeb's kinky desires? I knew all along that one was conditional to the other, so what did I want exactly?"

She waited for me to say something, then turned around and pretended to sleep. When I woke up in the middle of the night, only Adam was lying next to me and when she snuck back into the room early morning, I once again pretended to be asleep.

Our vacation-like work getaway came to an end. Back at the office, we gathered a hundred and twenty men and women whose characteristics matched our target audience. We segmented them into smaller groups and ran our edited images and videos by them. We asked them standard questions, "What do you see? How does it make you feel? Does it excite you to find out more about the product?"

About eighty-five percent of the men answered that they wanted to have that car, woman, and house in that exact order. Ten percent asked about the product and five percent asked what was in it for the bank. "What's the catch?"

The majority of the women said they wanted to be as content and complete as the woman in the picture, and a few asked what was in it for the bank.

We were happy; we achieved our goal, which was to make people say, "I want to be that family." The rest, we knew, we would make happen with the right timing, words, and music.

On Tuesday, the twentieth of September 2022, as I sit on my kitchen floor and reflect on that part of my life, I realize I did to Lara exactly what Waheeb had done to her. I took from her what I wanted and temporarily humored the rest. I empathized with her pain because she reminded me of my sister, and once I had my successful campaign, Lara and all her stories became irrelevant. I too looked at that billboard and wanted to be the woman with long, wild hair in a flowing white dress, expensive open-toe sandals, red lipstick, and a big happy smile. I wanted a husband who would negotiate with a bank, get a loan, buy me a big house, and take me on drives along the coast in a convertible.

I did not call Zayn that first time because I was worried that he might call the police and put out a search party. I did so because I was tired. I was tired of standing on a sidewalk in painful shoes, waiting for a taxi in the heat. I was tired of going home to aging parents and eating cold okra that my mother left out for me. I was tired of being alone. I asked Zayn all the right questions, then told him exactly what he needed to hear. I knew exactly which parts of the day to call and when to end the call. I was an expert at selling ideas, so I sold him the idea that we were perfect for each other, and while at it, I convinced myself I was in love with him and could not live without him.

The face all over the media today is Yasmeen; an independent, strong woman, an owner of a bakery in our neighborhood. She is a middle-aged mother of four, her hair is tied up in a neat bun, and she wears a comfortable oversized white shirt, loose jeans, and pink sneakers. This woman is not modeling to be Yasmeen; she is her. I know because I have been to her bakery many times. On one occasion, I followed my children in while on a phone call arguing with a supplier. Mo asked for a chocolate muffin, and Elena pointed at a strawberry tart. I waited by the cashier. Yasmeen punched in the total, looked at me with pity, and handed me a complimentary almond croissant.

Not for a second did I wish I was her. Not because I often saw her mopping the floor or scratching her head, trying to figure out bills, and rushing to lock the store so she could pick her kids up from school, but because baking was not my thing. I hated how flour got between your nails, how precise you needed to be with ingredients, and mostly because I always pulled those biscuits out of the oven too soon.

There was a time when marriage was a declaration of independence. Two people decided it was time for them to create a world of their own, a world separate from the one that surrounded them, and a world where they made and broke the rules because it was no one's business how they did things in their family.

A power-struck man who was obsessed with wealth usually found himself a wife who, more than anything, was fond of big diamonds and pretty things. She was happy as long as he spoiled her with luxury and gifts, and he was happy as long as she looked at him like he was the greatest man on earth. A man who took life too seriously and came home beaten up by its burdens took a wife who shared his miserable views. She spent her days kneading dough, and evenings listening to him mope. A carefree hippy, if I may, married a free spirit and wandered joyfully through life. Outside their lives together, these men and women were exposed to a very limited number of people or events. They shared their experiences with each other because how else would they spend their evenings? So, they both evolved together in the same direction and under the same influence. They loved each other because they made each other happy.

Their souls belonged to God, and they believed that only in heaven when they were nothing but a soul, would they rest with their true soulmates for all eternity? Here on earth, their spouses were nothing but a companion who walked with them through an inevitable destiny.

Sure, some of those marriages might not have ended well, but I believe that was a much better tactic than the one we adopt today: marrying someone just because we are physically attracted to them. Nowadays, you will see a minimalist miserably married to a workaholic, or carefree hippie married to a serious accountant, just because they believed they loved each other and could compromise their way through life trying to make each other happy. He goes with her on a hike; she sits through that dreadful movie. She watches the kids while he goes on that business trip. He comes home, and she is drained, so he offers to give her a girls' night out while he bathes and puts the kids to bed. Soon, life finds balance; they are both equally invested and run out of transactions.

In a time when it is becoming easier to physically distance ourselves from people, it is also becoming easier to have a soul-touching conversation with anyone at any time. How then are we expected to stay tuned-in and fully invested in a relationship with someone just because we decided at one point in time that they could be *the one*?

So, we grant exclusive rights over our bodies to our spouses while our souls wander the workplace, social media, online games, and enjoy the company of several temporary soulmates.

I think of all the mornings that I woke up happy in the warmth of Zayn. In between meetings throughout the day, I would make myself a cup of coffee, lean back on my chair, open my phone, and watch a fair number of thirty-second videos. In those fifteen minutes, I told my subconscious at least two things my husband was not doing right. In the evenings, we both sat on a sofa and instead of sharing our experiences together, we each stared at a hundred different videos on our respective phones. My phone told me, "If your man does not look at you the way Jonathan looks at Emily, he is not the one." I'm pretty sure Zayn's phone told him things like that too, only his phone knew he was a man, probably never showed him that video of Jonathan and Emily, and must have told him I was not good enough for him. Let alone all the things we now believed we wanted, that we never knew existed. Just like that, Zayn and I were two very different people than the ones who woke up next to each other in the morning. We did not evolve together or in the same direction. I cannot even claim with any certainty that we were evolving; our minds were in constant fluctuation and most likely deteriorating.

Back in the day, we advertisers used to create thirty-second teaser videos. We aired these short blimps a few weeks before launching our full three-minute advertising video. The purpose of these teasers was to prepare our target audience for the actual campaign and guarantee that when we hit, they watched with full attention, and their minds absorbed our message. Then we went back to flooding media channels with short and long stories featuring our product because we knew that if someone was exposed to our ads at least once, our product was bound to linger somewhere in their minds.

This was no modern-day discovery, you see; humans knew all along that stories, scriptures, and images are bound to influence people's actions.

The ancient school of yoga claims that dissatisfaction and suffering are caused by ignorance, which is further explained to be caused by misconception, lack of knowledge, or false knowledge. This can be traced back to *Samskaras*, imprints in the subconscious. It is believed that everything a human is ever exposed to, starting as early as when they are conceived and still in their mother's womb, leaves an imprint on the subconscious. As do other experiences: the knowledge one accumulates from their surrounding environment, culture, and information passed on by parents, and trauma we inherit in the DNA that we carry from ancestors we never met. Now imagine how many imprints are left on our subconscious when we spend five minutes watching three hundred videos. How many influencers tell us what our lives should look like? How many one-line philosophical musicals do we allow to sink in without ever finding out the whole version which tells us who this philosopher is? Which era did they belong to, or what the context of their true message was? How many of these quotes change the course of our day, week, or month?

The answer to how I got here, and why my marriage looked the way it did, was my deliberate ignorance. I knew more than anyone how the media works, but at times chose to see only what I wanted to see. I mean look, I am relatively smart and when I was willing to admit it, I knew if your man did not look at you the way Jonathan looked at Emily, it only meant that you were not the one, and not the other way around. After all, he was looking at her, while she was staring into the abyss. Once I acknowledged this truth, I no longer allowed that image to linger in my head and moved on to the next one.

I wonder how much of my life was planned by the people who control the media, the people who create dreams out of Laras. Is this house the home I really want for myself? Which campaign advertising a baby clothing brand manipulated me into believing I wanted children? I never hugged my nephews or took them out for ice cream. I did not feel like anything was missing from my life when I saw Adam. I did not enjoy holding my babies through sleepless nights or changing their diapers. I did not have the patience to walk them through their tantrums. I wanted that smiling girl with a big afro and cute boy in that fancy stroller, and a pacifier in his mouth. I wore clothes designed for working women my age, even when I was resting at home. I made reservations at restaurants that had cars like ours parked outside, but I don't know if I really liked the food. We vacationed in towns that popped on our screens as top destinations. We were happily married when it was a thing and I think maybe the reason I am unhappy now is because… remember that client of mine? The bank! They decided it was better if women bought their own houses because they believed two loans were better for their business than one.

I imagined Oyoun Almaha in the kitchen with me. She did

not pay much attention to me, sitting there on the floor. She opened a drawer and realigned some forks and spoons, then opened a cabinet and ran her finger through a pot, checking for grease.

"Mama," I called out to her.

"Yes?" She looked at me.

"Am I having a mid-age crisis?"

"No! You are just all grown up and realize there is no one to blame for your ignorance but yourself. It is time you question whether everything you believed was worth pursuing truly was so. Whether everything that upset you was truly worth it, and that, the thought that maybe it was not and that you were wrong all along, hurts your pride, so you want to call it a crisis. Many people do. They just wait for their awakened awareness to go back to sleep and continue to live the second half of their lives with the same ignorance as the first. The choice is yours."

"Do you think women are ever going to be equal to men?" I whined.

"For you to grant people equal rights to things, you must first be able to look at people with equal eyes, which is something we fail to do. We do not even look at man and man equally. We brush away a Ghalib's worship-like love, weigh it on a scale of social stigma, while we compare Kareem's lust to God's satisfaction. We women do not look at women and men equally. We declare a Nargis has gone through enough and created a human barrier between her and any discomfort, while the only way Lara's pain could ever be acknowledged is if she wrapped herself in her offender's sins and marched with a flag that announced, *Me Too*.

You are upset because your husband did not wait for you at the dinner table. You are upset because he did not celebrate your success, right?"

"Yes."

"When your father came home every night after a long day at work, he did not think, '*I had a hard day and am exhausted,*' but '*I will wait for my wife before I start eating because she has an equal right over this food.*'"

He thought, *Poor Oyoun Almaha must have had a long day taking care of the house, the children, and cooking. Come, Oyoun Almaha, let us have something to eat and rest together.*

When the builder across my window was building a house, I did not say to myself, "*What the hell is this man doing? Given the opportunity, I could do a better job than him*, and what did I care what the arch or pillars looked like? I was most likely never going to step foot in that house, but I spent a couple of minutes showing him interest because I believed the poor man worked so hard not only building a house that was safe but also tried his best to make it as beautiful as possible, so his work deserved a little admiration. And you know what? I am pretty sure he brought down those pillars and lifted the arch because he thought that the poor lady in the window deserves to feel like the view she looks at every day is something she would want to admire. I believed the man pushing the tomato cart needed to feel what he was doing was important. He did not grow those tomatoes, nor did he own a fancy store, but still, he deserved to feel like he had important work to do and that his customers had expectations from him. He probably believed the highlight of this woman's day is buying tomatoes, how proud she must feel when she finds a good pick. How it must change her cooking experience; she deserves the best quality, and so he tried harder every day.

"We were not created equal creatures, my child. Some of us are more daring, others less ambitious, some more conscious than others, some more inclusive, others more selfish. Maybe we were never meant to attain equality; maybe the true test was how altruistic we could be.

"In your chase for equality, you left behind altruism. What if it is time to admit that you have invested enough time and effort in this chase? What if you try altruism instead? And equal opportunities might just naturally follow suit."

All Lives Matter

Not so long ago, the kids and I went to see my mother on a Friday afternoon. She smothered us with hugs and kisses, then excitedly said, "Mohammed, Elena, come with me." My mother always used Mo's full name and hated that we replaced his auspicious name, Mohammed, with a nickname. I followed them upstairs to a corner table in her bedroom. There was a wooden box placed on the table like a treasure. I had not been to my mother's bedroom in ages, but recognized that box right away. It was the box where she stored all her Qura'an books. She opened the lid, unraveled the sequenced velvet cover, and my kids were in awe.

"Teta! They are so pretty," said Elena. Mo picked one of the Qura'an books up, admired it, kissed it, and gently placed it back. "Take one, each of you. Anyone you like, and every time you read it, pray for me, and all your grandparents. May Allah rest their souls," she told them with a big smile. They spent some time examining the beautiful covers and different styles of calligraphy before they made their selection. We had a few copies of the Qura'an at home, but they were the standard green hard covers we rarely picked up to read. My kids have applications on their iPads where they can also listen to the verses, making it easier for them to memorize at school.

Ever since I can remember, my mother ventured across town a week before Ramadan to buy a new copy of the Qura'an. She made sure her new one had a different design and color than the ones she already owned and tried her best not to buy from the same vendor twice because she believed that he too would be rewarded by Allah every time she read, and she wanted to grant that opportunity to as many people as possible.

We headed downstairs to a display of biscuits and cake; my mother went to the kitchen to fetch her teapot that had been cooking on a slow fire. When she came back, my children had their copies of the Qura'an sitting on their laps while they stared at their phones. She gave me *the look*; I jumped to my feet, picked up the books, kissed the covers, asked Allah to forgive us, and gently placed them on a high shelf with respect. The kids were too consumed to notice anything had happened, and because Oyoun Almaha believed one should never judge, or undermine a mother in front of her children, she whispered in my ear low enough for them not to hear, "Teach them something." I apologetically nodded my head and lowered my gaze.

"So, what important business are you running on your phones? I hope you are not missing any important meetings. How many employees are messaging you? Tell them to at least give you Fridays off so you can spend some time with your grandmother. Tell them she is old and only God knows if she will still be here next week." She teased Mo and Elena as she poured us some tea.

"Teta, we were just posting something to support the All Lives Matter movement," Mo whined.

"Look, this is what Mama posted." Elena showed my mother the post I shared with a lengthy caption underneath.

"*All Lives Matter*, I like this phrase," she answered pausing for a moment before she recited a verse from the Qura'an in Arabic, which translates into:

"*O ants, enter your dwellings that you not be crushed by Solomon and his soldiers while they perceive not. Solomon smiled, amused and said, 'My Lord, enable me to be grateful for your favor which you have bestowed upon me and upon my parents and to do righteousness of which you approve. And admit me by your mercy into the ranks of your righteous servants.'"*

"Do you know the story of Sayedna Sulayman?" she asked.

"A little, but you tell us, Teta," Mo answered.

Elena shook her head, slid down to the floor, and sat cross-legged next to my mother's feet in full attention.

"Sayedna Sulayman was not much older than you when he accompanied his father, the great King Dawood, on his court, where people from all across the kingdom came to present their disputes and ask for justice. One day, a farmer complained that his neighbor's sheep strayed into his fields and destroyed the vineyard that he had spent a whole year planting and caring for. The king fell into a long silence, trying to find a way the poor shepherd could compensate for the farmer's loss. Sulayman asked permission to speak, and when granted, he suggested that the shepherd work on the farm for a year and restore the damage his sheep caused, while the farmer would keep the sheep and benefit from its wool and milk that year and when things found balance, each would reclaim their rightful property. The king and all his council were impressed by the young man's wisdom.

Soon after, the king summoned his nineteen sons in front of all the kingdom's chiefs and scholars and put them to a test by asking them some challenging questions:

What one thing remains closest to man?

What is the farthest from his reach?

What two matters are inseparable?

What phenomenon does a man witness that leaves him in awe each and every time?

What are the two things that shall remain unchanged until

the end of time?

What two things will always be different?
What things are opposites of each other?
What act shall always result in good?
Which action always results in bad?

All the king's sons, chiefs, and scholars were left speechless. No one had answers to the king's riddling questions. After giving them enough time to contemplate, King Dawood looked at Sulayman and ordered him to speak. Sulayman stood up and said:

The thing constantly lingering close to man is death.

The farthest from his reach is the past-time that shall never return.

Body and soul are inseparable.

The phenomenon that shall always leave man in awe is the sight of a body without a soul.

The sky and earth are the two things that shall remain unchanged.

Day and night are always different.

Life and death are opposites.

Patience is the act which always results in good and haste in a time of anger in bad.

Sulayman's answers confirmed the King's prophesy, and so he announced him, his youngest son, to be the successor to his throne. God chose Sulayman to be more than just a king. He chose him to be a Prophet, and the mightiest man to ever walk on the face of earth and granted him divine powers. Sulayman was able to command the wind; he had a staff with which he controlled the jinn and demons. He ruled the seas and skies and spoke to animals that followed his every order.

One morning, he noticed one of his birds, a *hud hud,* was missing. He got upset and promised to punish the bird upon its return. But when the *hud hud* came back, he pleaded with the King and told him he had made an important discovery. A kingdom ruled by a wise woman, who somehow was misled to worship the sun. King Sulayman believed it was his duty to bring the Queen back to the right path and to the worship of no one but the one and only Allah. So, he wrote her a letter that began with the phrase; *"In the name of the almighty Allah."* Queen Balqees received his letter, which threatened that she must renounce her worship of the sun and to stop misleading her people, or King Sulayman would march toward them with an army whose might she could not begin to conceive. She sought counsel from her ministers who did not wish a king to bring destruction to their kingdom and believed they were not equipped to go to war against an army of whose magnitude they were unaware. Thus, they tried to persuade the King with valuable gifts, which he refused. Then, Queen Balqees decided she would pay him a visit herself. When he heard she was coming, Sulayman asked his soldiers who among them could bring him the Queen's throne before her arrival. An *Ifrit* claimed he could present it to the King before His Highness had a chance to get off his seat; another said he could bring it in the blink of an eye, which he did. The Mighty King did not allow himself to be taken over by pride; instead, he took a moment to humbly thank Allah for granting him the powers he possessed.

  The queen arrived and was astonished to find her throne there before her. Sulayman sensed that she had begun to believe that there was some truth to his claims and that there was a power higher than her perception. He invited her to step into his palace: she lifted her skirt, thinking she was about to step into water but then realized it was glass. Sulayman explained to Balqees that all this grandeur she had witnessed was granted to him by the almighty Allah. She accepted that she was mistaken to worship the sun and joined Islam.

The King led his army through mountains and deserts, and then suddenly heard a voice. An ant was warning its tribe to take cover lest Sulayman and his men crush them under their hooves. The great king came to a halt and stopped his soldiers; he got off his ride, smiled and kneeled down, reassuring the ants that their colony was safe. He ordered his army to change route, thanked Allah, and asked him to always guide him to the path of righteousness.

The Great King and Prophet lived a life full of wonders and ruled a kingdom like none before or after. He died leaning on his staff, which held his body upright. His army of Jinn, who claimed to be aware of all the secrets of life, had no idea he was dead and continued to serve him long after, until an ant chewed on his staff and his body fell to the ground.

Enough now, if you don't stop your Teta, she will go on forever. "Tell me, what is this movement, *All Lives Matter* about?"

Elena, my little version of Oyoun Almaha and quite the storyteller herself straightened her back, looked at her grandmother intensely, and said, "Four policemen were filmed on a street in America as they assaulted an African American man. One of them pressed his knee against the man's neck while he lay on the floor. The man kept telling them he could not breathe until he died. He was only forty-six years old. People are upset and demand the officer is punished. They started a movement, 'Black Lives Matter,' but then others from different ethnicities also shared stories where policemen abused their power and unrightfully harassed them because they were a minority."

"What did he do? Why were the police arresting him?" my mother asked.

"I don't know," Elena answered.

"Mohammed, do you know?"

"No, but it does not matter. What matters is how he died," he answered.

"Yes, murder is wrong and no one, police officer or otherwise, is allowed to take a life or even physically assault someone, but it does matter what kind of a life this man lived, what kind of a life led to the moment where a forty-six-year-old was being arrested. If a thousand people join this movement, it would be nice if two hundred made sure the government was doing its job right and demanded justice for the man's death, while maybe eight hundred could look around and make sure all lives, that were still alive, mattered. It is important to honor the lives of the living just as much as we honor the dead. Don't you think?" She went quiet for a moment, then changed the subject, "How's school?"

"School makes no sense. We can learn everything we want on our phones," Mo whined.

"Really?"

"Yes, what do we learn at school that we cannot learn off the internet?"

"Well, you learn to endure twenty other people from different backgrounds and upbringings for seven hours straight. No matter how annoying your classmates are, you sit with them in a room throughout the day, you work with them, play football with them, eat with them, and I am pretty sure plan mischief and get in trouble with them. You learn to respectfully listen to your teacher speak for forty-five minutes, even if the topic does not interest you much. These are all skills your phone, or the internet will never be able to teach you. And if you don't go to school, how would you have learned that the morning sun was refreshing, and the afternoon sun burning?" I was relieved to hear my mother, who once was not so enthusiastic about the educational system, say this to my children.

I Googled George Floyd when I got home because I was not comfortable with the thought that I only cared about his life after he was dead, sinking into my skin. But more so, because I was scared of my mother, and believed I got lucky and escaped her that day. She could have asked me the same question she asked my kids, and there is no way she would have let me off the hook as easily. I had no idea he was born in North California and grew up in Texas. I still don't know why he moved and under what circumstances. I did not know he played football and basketball through high school and college. How good he was and why did he stop? Did he choose to stop, or was he forced to give up his passion for sports to support his family? I had no idea he had been convicted for eight crimes between 1997 and 2005, what those crimes were, and was he rightfully or wrongfully accused. If he had committed those felonies, what life conditions forced him to do so? I had no idea he had lost both his jobs during the Covid-19 pandemic and what went through his mind when he went into that store to buy cigarettes on the day he lost his life.

On another curb closer to my country, a mother sang at the top of her lungs as she paraded her son, "Hela hela hey, hela hela hey, hayyu Mohammed, hela hela hey, hela hela hey." Neighbors heard her voice coming from a place that had surpassed the most painful alleys of agony and had nowhere left to go but dance in joy and joined her celebration. Some came with drums, some with firecrackers, and others with snacks.

A kiosk owner donated a hundred sandwiches to feed the

crowd before he ran out of bread as more and more people gathered on the street. They cheered for the boy and yelled, "Welcome, Mohammed. Welcome, our hero."

"Mohammed, our neighborhood hero."

"Mohammed, the pride of Shaikh Jarrah."

Passersby waved; taxi drivers stopped to shake his hand. He kept walking in his bright green sweatshirt with a big smile and squinted eyes, waving back at his audience with utmost kindness.

At first sight, I mistook the twenty-five-year-old Mohammed in the video for a sixteen-year-old boy. He looked as old as my Mo. Turns out he just has one of those faces that carried out the same innocent features as he aged. I swiped up with my thumb and saw him again in another video, his mouth and eyes wide open, screaming in terror as four soldiers ganged up on him and cornered him on the street. People tried to pull the soldiers back; they tried to come between them and the young man. "He has a condition, please. Be gentle," they begged. "He has Down Syndrome; he does not fully understand why you are doing this."

"I'm sure he did not mean to look at you like that," an old man pleaded as the soldiers lifted Mohammed by his shoulders and legs. Then, one of them noticed they were being filmed by more people than they could apprehend and advised his fellow soldiers to release the boy. Mohammed ran to the old man's arms, and I don't know if that old man was his father, a relative, or just a stranger from the street, but he held him tight and cried.

The next day, Mohammed's mother paraded her son down the street. She most likely did so to help him overcome his fear and step out again. There was an outburst from the people of Palestine or Jerusalem, whatever you wish to call that part of earth on which humans, just like us, breath, walk, and try to sleep. "Men, women, and children are wrongfully assaulted by officials here every single day. What about us?" they called out on social media. I saw these posts, felt a pinch in my heart, allowed my eyes to tear up a little, and swiped up.

Mohammed Al Ajlouni still walks those streets and most likely comes face to face with the same soldiers; he is still alive under those same circumstances. There are probably many more men and women who still live under the same or worse circumstances all over the world today. I don't rally for the quality of their lives; I don't post anything on my social media, and I don't stop to make sure their colonies are safe. You know why? George Floyd's life did not really matter to me. What mattered to me was that a man of the law in the United States of America crossed the line, and when a year later he was sentenced to twenty-two and a half years in prison, I was relieved. Because chances are, somewhere in the near future my children might come to me and say they want to go to MIT or UCLA. I won't be able to stop them, and I want them to be safe. So, unless officers like Derek Chauvin were punished and set as an example, it would have been an open invitation to all other officers to do as they please and I would not be able to comfortably send my kids to a country like that. What are the chances my kids or anyone I care about would ever say they want to go to Palestine or Jerusalem to study? And there is no Disney World there, so.

I know how it sounds, but how are we to ever change if we are not willing to be honest with ourselves?

*

We were driving home after praying Eid at our neighborhood mosque. Elena sat in the front seat next to her father; she loosened up her headscarf, revealing some of her hair. "Elena! Please, take that scarf off," I said as though she had done something terribly wrong, and because she never argued with me in the presence of her father, she immediately took it off and stuffed it in her handbag. Zayn gave me a baffled look but did not ask. From where I was sitting and the way she had that scarf half hanging on her head, she looked like a girl I saw on the news. A young girl with the same hair color and skin tone as her, just a few years older, and a girl who had been shot in the face because she wanted to go to school.

Men created the educational system to contain information they decided important and locked it up in what they called schools. They then chose to only allow boys into these schools. Boys came out years later, calling themselves graduates. They looked down on their mothers, sisters, and wives for not knowing how to read, write, or decipher a numeric equation, and they picked on them and teased them. Fed up with being unable to earn a respectful living, women demanded a share of this pie that men had baked only for themselves.

We witnessed many years of failed arguments:

"A girl is as intelligent as a boy."

"A woman needs to be able to provide for her family in case her husband does not return from war."

"How is an uneducated woman supposed to raise educated men?"

"Women are half the society. How would a country prosper if you leave them behind?"

Until one day, someone suggested, "If you want to win this election, grant women the right to vote, and then promise them schools for girls," and just like that, girls were allowed to go to school. I was under the presumption this was a story I would never have to tell my daughter; the history of how girls were granted the right to go to school was forgotten past. I believed the ugliest war a girl had to fight for an education in modern times was the one I had with my mother twenty years ago. Then, I saw Malala Yousafzai on the screen of my television.

She lived on a picturesque mountain, beautiful enough to make a cover for a postcard if people had still used those. On that same mountain, also stood a man with a gun in his hand. He claimed he had picked the weapon up to protect religion. This man also happened to have a premonition that all the women in their town became teachers and doctors, and the army of faith starved to death because they had no one to cook their *daal* and *roti*. So, he declared it *haram* for girls to go to school.

Young Malala wrapped her scarf around her head and stepped out; maybe she believed these uncles would succumb to her sweet stubbornness. She was, after all, the daughter of a brave man who had spent years fighting for the same cause. But these men, who were supposed to be protecting her borders and faith, threatened to kill her if she did not stop provoking girls to ask for their right to dream. "I think of it often and imagine the scene clearly. Even if they come to kill me, I will tell them what they are trying to do is wrong, that education is our basic right," she said, when she envisioned coming face to face with them.

While she sat amongst her peers in a classroom one day, squeezing her mind to answer questions on an exam paper she studied so hard for. The army of faith, grown men in turbans and beards gathered in another room and spent hours discussing how the devil had taken the form of a girl, and if not stopped, it would corrupt the minds of the whole town. Since all their threats on television, radio, newspapers, and Facebook had failed, one of them announced that they were forced to act. And just like that, a few leaders of many followers decided it was time to kill her.

A man hiding behind a mask stopped the bus that she was riding home on, yelled out for her to identify herself, and shot her. The bullet traveled from her left eye through her neck and landed in her shoulder. The soldier did not stand over her body in glory claiming his victory, instead, he disappeared into thin air.

Malala was hospitalized, and when stable enough, transferred to England for more treatment. She became the most famous teenager in the world. The whole world condemned the actions of these men and offered to stand by her. The young girl went to school and graduated college in England. She was granted many prizes and awards for her bravery, and once again comes face to face with men who dress and sound exactly like the man who shot her. She still pleads with them for the safety of girls who, just like her, want nothing but to one day play an important role in their communities.

I watch this well-composed girl stand so calmly, repeatedly demanding the same thing again and again, not for herself but for girls she may not even know. Why does she still have to stand there? Why does she still come face-to-face with monsters that not only peeked from under her door but could have actually killed her? Why did none of us grown-ups say, *It's okay child, we will take it from here, you have been through enough.* Would she even trust us with this mission that obviously matters to her more than her own life?

On this same planet, a girl not much younger than Malala, and who looks nothing like her, denounces her right to go to school. Not because it is dangerous. Her school is perfectly safe, welcoming, and for most kids her age, even fun. Instead, on Fridays, while her friends plan sleepovers and trips to the mall, she sits on the pavement in front of a parliament building.

Throughout history, humans repeatedly lost their way, and corrupt rulers, blinded by greed, presented the people with lifeless idols to worship, demanding they sacrifice a good sum of their little earnings in return for security and food. When things got really bad, God sent a prophet to lead these people back to light. To put the people's faith to a true test, these prophets usually emerged from the most unlikely of places. The prophet revealed a miracle, and the people who needed political protection the most were usually the first to abandon their idols and follow the prophet into the depths of danger. They spent day and night building an ark, despite there being no signs of a storm, and when the animals approached, they stepped aside, making way for the creatures to board first, as they were more essential to recreating a sustainable ecosystem. Despite this unexplainable flood of animals, the people still doubted a storm was coming and were only truly and completely convinced at the sight of that first raindrop.

Similarly, a little girl emerges from Sweden, a kingdom where the air is fresh and crisp, and where every season has a different color, and fights for the right for clean air. This girl is not a prophet. Well, because God told us he was not going to send any more messengers, and because she wears a yellow raincoat and jeans, not a beard and cloak.

Nonetheless, she is equipped with a miraculous superpower: the ability to single-mindedly focus on one message, and she comes with a prophecy. Sure, she does not quote a divine script from God or recite sentences we never heard before in a complicated language. She quotes facts the adults of her time presented to her on news channels which never lie and recites numbers we witness with our own eyes. She does not warn us of an inconceivable storm on a sunny day. She shows us burning forests and drowning villages. She skips school, the same right that her sister from another continent got shot in the face fighting for, and stands on the streets calling people to pay attention, to see the darkness they are about to bring upon themselves. Millions follow her. Unfortunately, these millions cannot make much of a difference unless we all stop worshipping our comfort.

When I first saw Greta Thunberg, I believed her smile was bound to charm humanity into doing better. A few years later, I saw her again, now a young woman shadowed with despair. The leaders of our time had once again invited her to speak at an important conference. "My message is that we'll be watching you," she started off in a tone we grown-ups use when we had been betrayed by the one we love the most so many times we give them one last chance. A tone we use when we want them to believe we are threatening them, but in reality, we are begging. We beg because if they betray us one more time, we will lose faith in all humanity.

The grown-ups in the room laugh, and then she continues, "This is all wrong. I shouldn't be up here. I should be back in school on the other side of the ocean. Yet you all come to us young people for hope?

How dare you?

You have stolen my dreams and my childhood with your empty words. And yet, I'm one of the lucky ones. People are suffering. People are dying. Entire ecosystems are collapsing. We are in the beginning of a mass extinction, and all you can talk about is money and fairytales of eternal economic growth.

How dare you?

For more than thirty years, the science has been crystal clear. How dare you continue to look away and come here saying that you are doing enough, when the politics and solutions needed are still nowhere in sight. You say you hear us and that you understand the urgency. But no matter how sad and angry I am, I don't want to believe that, because if you really understood the situation and kept on failing to act, then you would be evil. And that I refuse to believe.

The popular idea of cutting our emissions in half in ten years only gives us a fifty percent chance of staying below one-point-five degrees and the risk of setting off irreversible chain reactions beyond human control. Fifty percent may be acceptable to you, but those numbers do not include tipping points, most feedback loops, additional warming hidden by toxic air pollution or the aspects of equity and climate justice.

They also rely on my generation sucking hundreds of billions of tons of your CO_2 out of the air with technologies that barely exist.

So, a fifty percent risk is simply not acceptable to us - we who have to live with the consequences.

How dare you pretend that this can be solved with just business-as-usual and some technical solutions? With today's emissions levels, that remaining CO_2 budget will be entirely gone within less than eight and a half years. There will not be any solutions or plans presented in line with these figures today. Because these numbers are too uncomfortable, and you are still not mature enough to tell it like it is. You are failing us.

But the young people are starting to understand your betrayal. The eyes of all future generations are upon you, and if you choose to fail us, I say we will never forgive you.

We will not let you get away with this. Right here, right now, is where we draw the line. The world is waking up. And change is coming, whether you like it or not.

Thank you."

She was applauded like she was at many other conferences where they showered her with prizes, titles, and more promises. I saw her again, this time she gave them a title: "*So-called leaders,*" and dismissed their promises as "*blah, blah, blah.*" This version of Greta scared me. She looked and sounded like someone who had lost faith in all humanity. And what do our scriptures tell us happens next?

We witness these catastrophes on our televisions and phones. We know there are people out there whose homes have been swallowed by the sea and washed away by rain. We know there are children out there who live every day accepting in the back of their heads that a day will come when they will lose their perfect bedrooms with all their favorite toys to a fire. We know that we are losing most of our food sources to drought. All this girl is asking us to do is sacrifice a small sum of our extravagant conveniences so our grandchildren could have a planet as livable as the one we received.

Why doesn't this girl's life matter? What kind of life have we left her with after depriving her of a worry-free childhood, a dreamy future, and faith in the goodness of her own kind?

Forgive Me Child for I Have Sinned

When the horror of being a bad mother kicks me in the stomach, and the pain becomes unbearable, I recite a poem by the wise Khalil Gibran to comfort myself. It goes like this:

"Your children are not your children. They are the sons and daughters of life's longing for itself.

They come through you but not from you, and though they are with you, they belong not to you.

You may give them your love but not your thoughts, for they have their own thoughts. You may house their bodies but not their souls, for their souls dwell in the house of tomorrow which you cannot visit, not even in your dreams. You may strive to be like them, but seek not to make them like you. For life goes not backward nor tarries with yesterday.

You are the bows, from which your children as living arrows are sent forth. The archer sees the mark upon the path of the infinite and bends you with His might that His arrows may go swift and far. Let your bending in the archer's hand be for gladness; for even as He loves the arrow that flies, so He loves also the bow that is stable."

I took these words; *They come through you, but not from you* to heart and shielded my children from everything I thought to be backward thinking. I liberated myself and them from the fears that held our parents back, from dulling ideologies, teachings that limited their horizons, and the shackles of social expectations.

Like our children, a lot of other things also come through us and not from us. My campaigns, for example, don't come from me; they just pass through me. I take the words my clients use to describe their products, carefully observe them, understand them, find their deepest insights, and put together a set of attractive images, videos, and sounds. I spend days and nights visiting and revisiting my ideas, and only when I am completely in love with every aspect of a campaign do I present it to an audience and expect them to like it. A scientific discovery comes not from a scientist himself but through him. He collects data from his surroundings or made available to him by his predecessors, analyzes it, and comes to a theory. He does not share this theory with the world until he is confident that he has done all he could with it. An artist believes he is possessed by a higher spirit as his brush strokes against his canvas, and that he is just an instrument through which his art comes to life, and not that his art comes from him. Still, he works on his piece for weeks, months, and sometimes years, and carefully chooses to make it available only to the eyes of those who would truly appreciate it.

    Yet, somehow, I convinced myself that all my children required of me was nourishment and companionship. Nourishment, I translated in timed meals, clean clothes, good schools, gyms, and the latest electronics. Companionship, I labeled as quality time. The time I was not willing to give them when they interrupted my gossip session, excited to tell me something, when it meant having to postpone a meeting to attend an event at school or take them on a play date. Quality time was when I chose to take a day off work and take them to the beach so they could build a sandcastle as far away from me as possible, while I sunbathed and read a book. Quality time was when I chose to kick back on the sofa and watch a movie with them in silence.

I frequently manage to fail my children. I fail to surround them with healthy food choices. I am usually late for a soccer match and barely make it to a ballet recital. I lose my temper instead of helping them get through their tantrums. I snap at them for being too loud, too excited, or too upset. Every time this happened in the past, I lay in bed at night and beat myself up about it for hours, then tiptoed into their bedrooms, stroked their hair, kissed their sleeping eyes, and promised to do better the next day.

On Tuesday, the 20th of September 2022, I was under the impression that I had done better. I managed not to yell at them for fighting and had distracted them with an imaginary monkey instead. But was that really better? I sat on my kitchen floor and realized I once again owed my children an apology. Only this one was too heavy to carry upstairs. So, I imagined them there with me. A younger version of Mo, with his curly hair all messed up, his tiny hand wrapped around my fingers, sleeping on my lap, and baby Elena on my other lap with her soft straight hair, her right cheek gracefully resting on her right palm. I looked at them and whispered, "I have a confession to make…"

I came across a colorful store at the mall one afternoon. It felt nice to look at all those cute colors after being stuck in front of a laptop staring at numbers in a gray office, surrounded by people in black suits and white *thobes* all week. What drew me toward the store were the banners dangling from the ceiling. A picture of a sweet, sparkly smile and red plump cheeks had me mesmerized. It would be nice to have one of those in our house, I thought, and could not rid myself of that thought. My neck was stuck up, and I neglected looking down at what else the store held. Diapers, strollers, wipes, baby powder, lotions, and shampoos. I did not once ask myself if I was willing to uncomplainingly do all the work that came with having a baby.

Forgive me, my child, I have sinned. I lied. I told myself and the world that I had some sort of motherly instinct bubbling inside me. The truth is a mother's strongest instinct is to protect her children, not conceive them into a world full of uncertainties.

Forgive me, my child. I managed to child-proof my china cabinets and make-up drawers, but failed to clean my house before welcoming you home. The walls are still smeared with mixed emotions, and the floors look like a puppet show stage, covered in footprints of your father and me jumping right and left at the signal of the puppet masters who shaped the play of our materialistic world.

Forgive me, Mo. I made you believe in legends like Timur-E-Lang and Hercules, then introduced you to a world where there were no more worthy battles to glorify you. A world where you were bombarded with messages that you were no longer needed to protect or provide for your family. We surrounded you with images of women with swords, ruling kingdoms with no men, and others in suits conquering the business world. We were cautious not to label you naughty, a bully, or a liar, yet failed not to hint that you were the bad guy women needed to protect themselves from and keep in check. We demanded almost nothing of you, showed little faith in you, and left you nowhere to splendor, then we wondered why you were so carelessly wasting away on a beanbag, dwelling in a video game.

Forgive me, Elena, I dressed you up in fluffy tutus and sparkly tiaras, then told you to snap out of it. Told you it was time to take yourself seriously and to have so much self-respect that you intimidate a man who believes buying you a diamond is romantic. We then surrounded you with movies that told you it was the most beautiful feeling in the world. I am sorry we presented you with a distorted image of man and chose the very few abusive to represent them all. We scared you from love but failed to erase its necessity. We tell you it is okay to be alone, and then sell you an overpriced blanket to help with your anxiety. We tell you to chase your independence and that starting a family can wait, and when it is too late, we tell you having a baby is still possible. All you need to do is spend all your hard-earned money on technologies we invented. And if that does not work, we encourage you to choose a more humane option: adopt a child whose parents we blew up in an unexplainable war. Maybe that way you help us repent for our mistake.

Forgive me, my children, I saw the words of modern-day parenting jumping up and down my screen and shelves at bookstores and decided not to teach you to kiss your mother's hand. With that, I also forgot to place my hand on your head with a blessed prayer. I saw you jump up and down in front of the TV, a controller in your hand, and an unusual grin on your face, so I did not force you to stop playing and join the prayers at the mosque. But when your father called out your name, you were forced to drop everything and present yourself with a *"yes, baba."* I should have forced you to walk to and back from the mosque; perhaps on that walk, you might have contemplated a path to your own soul.

We saw shiny cars displayed at showrooms, worked hard to afford those cars, and now drove you around in them, neglecting to teach you that your body is equipped with enough strength and perseverance to walk to the corner store. Perhaps if we chose to walk instead of drive from time to time, we would have learned to treat our planet with a little more respect.

We repeatedly tell you that money cannot buy happiness, the same lie we tell the poor, so they happily continue to serve the wealthy. We tell you this lie to relieve ourselves from your expectations. We live a different lie, that money can buy security, when in truth the most insecure people live in the biggest of houses.

Forgive me, my children, I handed you smartphones at ages a little too young so I could have access to you at all times, but failed to teach you that in the palm of your hand, you held the wisdom of all sages, hakeems, scientists, poets, and philosophers. Not a device to entertain you with videos of people imitating monkey moves and sounds. I am sorry, my children; we promised not to push you in the direction of our unlived dreams or entangle you in our desires, but oh do we do so more than ever. We limit your horizons to what we show you on screens; you no longer have two parents tampering with your mind but a whole industry doing so.

Forgive me, my children, we have failed you. We claim to have achieved what no human has ever before us, but left our humanity behind. We leave you with nothing but chaos. While elders and children die of malnutrition, women are forced to leave their homes and become a vulnerable prey for the wicked, and while the planet roars and threatens us to swallow our grandchildren alive, the common man is busy utilizing his power and voice to debate whether men should be allowed to dress like women and which toilets they should be allowed to use. And I am sorry, but the world leaders are also too busy arguing back.

Some stories, my children, have been preserved across time, religions, languages, and cultures for a reason. Pay attention to those stories and learn from them. Build your own ark. This ark does not have to be built of logs and metal and does not need to sail in water. It does not have to make sense to anyone but you. This ark may exist only in your mind to save you from the flood of chaos we created. Allow into your ark only that which is good and necessary for a new world. A world you construct for yourselves and let the rest wash away with us. We have failed you, my children; we are not as great as we claim to be, and what is worse is that we are not so helpless either.

Sitting on my kitchen floor, I take a good look at the world today and realize how maybe things were better before. When we believed God was watching us from high up beyond the seventh sky. When we believed he was on a throne so magnificent, it was a sin to even think our small, insignificant minds could begin to imagine what it might look like. We believed he watched our every move and heard our every thought, and was prepared to instantly strike us with his fury. Before going to bed every night, we would beg him to forgive us if, despite being so cautious throughout the day, we may have unwillingly committed a sin that escaped our awareness. The next morning, we would thank him for granting us another day and promised to spend it righteously. The call to prayer was the only dominator of the day; every other transaction was scheduled around prayer times, and when we heard it, everything else had to wait for ten minutes. A man took one route to the mosque, greeting everyone on his way, and a different route on his way back. A man's absence was noticed at a prayer, and his friends and relatives went to check on him. People knew when their neighbors were in need without them having to say anything and helped them out discreetly. Sure, we were more inclined to fight radical wars in the name of faith, but even in the midst of the bloodiest battles, soldiers were reminded that elders, women, and children were off-limits. Emperors took responsibility for the well-being of all people who sheltered within the walls of their empire. They constantly tried to make sure that no poor was left hungry, or that no weak felt threatened. The fear of what they would answer God when questioned turned their hair gray, and their worrisome eyes circled in black. You see, we believed we would be held accountable for everything we were granted, our years, days, minutes, and the power to see, hear, speak, and walk.

Gradually, we evolved into believing that God was right here surrounding us, and that we sensed His presence in the wind, the skies, and trees. Little by little, we forgot about His fury and relied more and more on His forgiveness and mercy. Like we would with a family or friend. So what if a man allowed himself to consume alcohol at late hours of the night? We looked the other way and asked God to guide him to the right path. We disguised gambling and bribes as business. Not only did we loudly envy our neighbor, but we also shared portraits of our lives from the right angle to make sure people envied us. We decided some empires were more important than others. Not all life was sacred; we disguised murdering helpless elders and children as collateral damage and told ourselves collateral damage was forgiven.

In the same verse that listed all those sins, there was another sin which we hold higher than all others: the most unforgivable sin of all, adultery. Well, because adultery offends our feelings. Wait, wait, not our feelings! Adultery offends a man's pride. Because somehow, when a man gets married, his honor is transferred from him and all his deeds to the body of his wife. And bear in mind, his honor is more important than her life. So yes, if a man commits adultery, it is because his wife failed to satisfy him, but if she does so, she failed to protect her husband's honor and must be stoned to death, in this case, along with her lover. Unless he holds a high rank in society, then it is nothing but a rumor, and shame on you for spreading whispers about people's personal lives.

We decided we were spiritual and not religious; what does that even mean? If you sit on a mat, wear a beaded *mala,* and meditate, you are aware you have a spirit, and the man at the office somehow believes he is without one?

We decided that God would understand if we delayed a prayer because we were eating, even if our stomachs were about to explode. He would forgive us if we were too late to catch the prayer at the mosque because Netflix said there was just five minutes remaining for the movie to end, or we wanted to watch just one more episode, video or take one more go at trying to beat that level. God would understand if we ignored the call for prayer because we were in an important meeting, even if minutes later we took a smoking break. Slowly, convenience became more important than values, and with time, comfort became the dominator of our lives. We called the pride that came with righteousness *Ego* and detached ourselves from it, and while doing so, we also detached ourselves from the guilt that came with wrongdoing.

Now, we tell ourselves that God is within us. And guess what? Tell a man that God is within him many times, and he will allow himself to play God because you can't rid yourself of that ego so easily. The empires these few men build don't draw lines on maps; they don't have borders or walls. Their greatness is only witnessed in articles featuring *The Wealthiest People on the Globe.* They unleash upon the rest of us a set of algorithmic angels and Satans. These algorithmic Satans encourage us to pursue our desires with utmost greed. Not only that, but they decide for us what desires we desire the most, and we believe them. The angels try to remind us of our values from time to time, but we swipe our thumbs up and dismiss them.

We no longer recognize that some messages we see when we gaze into our phones first thing in the morning are good, and others not so much. How some ideas are meant to be met with open arms, contained, and made use of, while others we should watch through a screen and ignore as they disappear. Some videos clear the heavy air from lingering misconceptions, and others are pointless. I don't know how to teach my children what I don't know, and it scares me. I think life was better before when the only mystery was what God had not yet revealed to us. A God we had faith in. Not mysterious humans who, like us, don't really know how valuable what they want really is, or for how long they will still want it.

I heard Zayn switch off the TV and walk toward the kitchen. I nervously started to pick myself off the floor, then decided maybe I should not. Maybe it was time I spoke my heart, and we let out all the shadows we shoved under our expensive carpets. So, I stayed there on the floor. My husband walked in, looked at me, and I sensed the words, "What are you doing there? Is everything okay?" at the tip of his tongue; he paused, looked away, grabbed a glass, filled it with water, and then asked me, "Did you take a look at the hotels I sent you? Winter break is soon, and I want to make reservations before prices go up."

I picked up my phone, opened the links he sent me, looked at the beautiful pictures, and planned our luxury winter vacation.